This Orchard book belongs to

_____

_____

_____

Notes:
This book is for my mummy, who always takes very good care of me when I am poorly. ♡ sl

ORCHARD BOOKS
338 Euston Road, London NW1 3BH
Orchard Books Australia
Level 17/207 Kent Street, Sydney, NSW 2000

First published in 2007 by Orchard Books
First published in paperback in 2007

Text and illustrations © Sam Lloyd 2007

ISBN 978 1 84616 174 2

A CIP catalogue record for this book is available from the British Library.

2 4 6 8 10 9 7 5 3 1

Printed in Singapore

Orchard Books is a division of Hachette Children's Books

Kiss-it-Better Hospital

Doctor Miaow's BIG EMERGENCY

Sam Lloyd

ORCHARD BOOKS

It's another bright morning
at Kiss-it-Better Hospital,
and Woof is busy cleaning the
blue light on his ambulance.

Inside, Doctor Miaow is very busy.
There are lots of patients for
her to look after!

There are temperatures to take, heartbeats to listen to, baby bunnies to feed, and look at Monkey – what's he got stuck on his head this time?! My goodness, so much to do!
And now the phone is ringing!

"Hello," says Doctor Miaow. "This is Kiss-it-Better Hospital. How can we help?"

"Miaooooow! It's Tom Cat. I've fallen out of the apple tree and hurt myself. Please come quickly!"

"We'll be there right away!" says Doctor Miaow.

Doctor Miaow dashes outside.
"**Quick**, Woof! Tom Cat has had an accident and we must go and help him!"

"I'll start the engine," says Woof. "Let's go!"
They climb into the ambulance and off they zoom!

Nee-nar, nee-nar goes the siren.
"Faster, Woof! **Faster!**" says Miaow.
"Turn left here."

Doctor Miaow races over to Tom Cat.
"My leg hurts," he sobs.
Doctor Miaow gently looks at it.
"How did this happen?" she asks.
"I was chasing Mr Bird up the tree
and I slipped," cries Tom Cat.

"I think your leg is broken," says Miaow.
"You'll have to go to hospital."

Miaow and Woof carefully put Tom Cat onto a
stretcher and whisk him off to the ambulance . . .

... and Woof drives back to Kiss-it-Better Hospital as quickly as he can. Nee-nar, nee-nar!

Back at the hospital, Doctor Miaow takes an x-ray of Tom Cat's broken leg, then she puts a very special plaster on it to make it better.

"You shouldn't chase Mr Bird," says Doctor Miaow. "He's a lot smaller than you."
Tom Cat feels sorry.

"Oh dear," sighs Tom Cat. "I've hurt my leg, but I've hurt poor Mr Bird's feelings more. I hope he'll still be my friend."

But cheer up, Tom Cat, you've got a visitor!

Rat-a-tat-tat!

There's a knock at the door . . .

It's Mr Bird!

"I'm sorry I was mean to you,"
says Tom Cat.
"That's OK," says Mr Bird.
"Let's be friends again."
"Hooray!" cheers Tom Cat.

"Would you like to sign my plaster?"
asks Tom Cat.

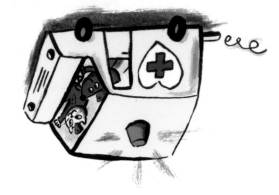